MW00955670

Evan Bunny

Story by
Gabriel Bench

Illustrations by
Pete Berg

© Matt Bench 2009

Text and Illustrations Copyright © 2009 by Matt Gabriel Bench

All rights reserved. No part of this book may be reproduced or transmitted in any form or by any means, electronic or mechanical, including photocopying, recording, video or by any information retrieval system, without permission from the copyright holder.

Printed in the U.S.A.

Library of Congress Control Number: 2009903727
ISBN #1-4392-3745-X

Published by:
Humble Bee Books
PMB A-3 · 621 SR 9 NE · Lake Stevens WA 98258

Evan Bunny:
Sequel to *Ester Bunny*. A winning story about pride, humility and second chances.

Upcoming Humble Bee Books include:
Ester Bunny: released 2008, A heartwarming and inspiring folk tale depicting the origin of the Easter Bunny.
Ella Bunny: Will hard times steal Ella's joy or will Ella rise to the occasion?
Purple Gold: An orphan boy's trials turns to gold.

To view the previews you may visit
www.humblebeebooks.com

 is

Dedicated to my sisters, Becky, Sandy, and Mary.
I have always felt their love and encouragement.

A special thank you to Pete Berg
for another wonderfully illustrated book.

A special thank you to my brother, Jeff Bench,
for editing Evan Bunny

A special thank you to Jen, Adam, Kim, Holly, and Josh
for providing great input to the story.

Most of all, thank you to my wife Sandy,
who truly is my better half.

.

**The Brookville Easter Parade
bubbled with activities —**
clowns riding unicycles, bands playing
lively music, balloons swaying, and
children laughing.

The gleeful crowd cheered as the Mayor awarded Ester a shiny certificate of courage and proclaimed her the official Easter Bunny. The Mayor then pulled back a tarp to unveil a beautiful bronze statue of Ester carrying a basket filled with colorful Easter eggs. The cheers grew as Ester was showered with a rainbow of streamers.

The Mayor hushed the cheering crowd and spoke, saying, "Ester showed great courage in using her unique God-given talents to follow her dreams of being a great artist. Even when others greatly discouraged her, she still succeeded."

The Mayor ended his speech by saying, "In honor of Ester Bunny, each year, just before Easter, a contest will be held to select a bunny who best represents Ester's character and talents to be that years official Easter Bunny." The cheers from the crowd erupted once again, lasting several minutes as the parade came to a close.

Ester was often asked what it was like to be the first Easter Bunny.

Ester was quick to say how grateful she was for a wise bunny named Golden whose help and encouragement was so important when other bunnies were not nice to her. She also would explain, though it wasn't always easy for her, everything, both easy and hard, had to happen in just the right order and at just the right time for her to become the Easter Bunny.

She was quoted as saying, "I could not have planned a better ending if I had tried. I was truly blessed."

Easter egg hunts became so popular that bunnies became instant superstars. The bunny selected official Easter Bunny for the year was treated like royalty.

Remaining humble is hard when so much honor and attention gets heaped on a bunny. The Easter Bunny was pampered and groomed. He would also hear praise like, "Easter Bunny, oh how beautiful you are", "We love you", and "Can we have your pawto-graph?"

Imagine trying to remain humble if you were Ester's grandson. Well, Evan was just that bunny.

You see, Evan was Ester's grandson and he was a glorious looking bunny. His features were very handsome. His fur shone like an auburn sun and felt as soft as a gentle breeze.

From the day he was born, Evan often heard that he was sure to be crowned the official Easter Bunny one day.

Evan was known for being good hearted. However, because of all of the special attention, he started to think he was more special than other bunnies. He started expecting everyone to give him special treatment and started to take his friends for granted. Can you imagine a bunny barking? Well, Evan's demanding voice sounded like he was barking out orders to his friends.

"Mic, fetch me some berries! Lollamore, brush my fur! White Cloud, get me something to eat!" Evan stopped listening to others, including his friends. He thought, 'why waste my time listening to them when what I have to say is much more important'?

Of course, what Evan had to say was not more important and he was wrong to treat his friends badly. As a result he lost many friends.

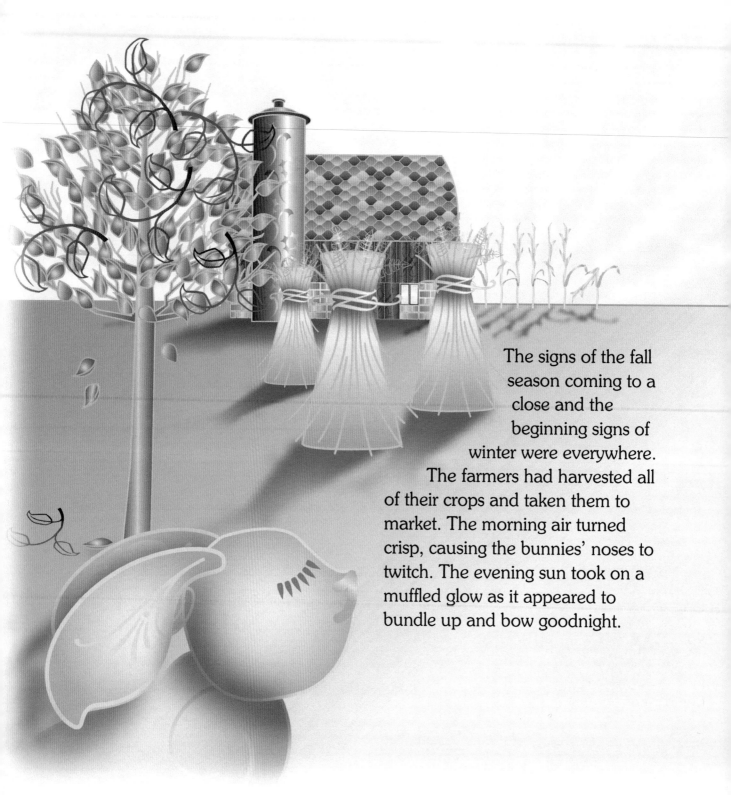

The signs of the fall season coming to a close and the beginning signs of winter were everywhere. The farmers had harvested all of their crops and taken them to market. The morning air turned crisp, causing the bunnies' noses to twitch. The evening sun took on a muffled glow as it appeared to bundle up and bow goodnight.

As winter swept in, excitement arose when those bunnies who had dreams of being crowned the next official Easter Bunny came from near and far to attend the Fine Bunny Academy. Here, bunnies were taught what they needed to know when competing for the crown and most importantly, the expectations of the official Easter Bunny.

Fine Bunny
Academy

During training, the bunnies learned how to sit up straight; how to hop gracefully; how to give a friendly wave to the crowd with their ears; how to groom their fur; how to paint eggs; how to quickly hide eggs without being seen, and how to talk about their reasons for wanting to be the next official Easter Bunny.

The expectations of the official Easter Bunny, better known as "C" training, were also taught. "C" training stood for character, commitment, and courage. Bunnies would learn the importance of being humble, being giving and not greedy, and having the courage to always do the right thing.

A crowd gathered as a parade of Easter Bunny hopefuls hopped by to enroll in the Fine Bunny Academy. Eyes throughout the crowd widened and jaws fell open in amazement at how beautiful the bunnies were. The hopefuls included Lilly Lop from Longview; Heather Hare from over the hill; Sandy Bunny from Frontier Village; Fin Rabbit from across the water, and many others. As grand as these bunnies were, they were no match for Evan. But where was Evan?

Evan had decided he was too good for the Fine Bunny Academy. He figured it was just a waste of time, because he was sure to win anyway.
Pride had overcome him.

The Fine Bunny Academy training finished just in time for the Easter Bunny contest. The contest began with all the bunnies hopping by, waving and smiling. Heather's and Lilly's furs were so shiny that their coats appeared to glow. Even without the special training, Evan's coat looked wonderful. All the bunnies showed their special talents. Laddy from Larue hid his eggs so fast and skillfully that the judges did not even notice he had started before he was done. Fin's egg coloring ability was really special. Only Evan with the training he received from Ester was able to match Fin in egg coloring. The events came to a close.

The scores were added and five finalists were selected. The finalists were Heather, Lilly, Fin, Laddy, and Evan. In turn, each bunny was asked,

"Why do you want to be the official Easter Bunny?" Heather said it was a life long dream of hers. Lilly talked about the joy of making people happy. Fin described his wish to be a role model. Laddy simply stated it would be a lot of fun. It was Evan's contest to win. With a heartfelt answer the crown would be his. The question was asked, "Evan, why do you want to be the official Easter Bunny?" Evan's pride welled up as he said, "Because I am the best and I deserve it".

The final votes were in. The Mayor himself read the results.

With a loud clear voice the Mayor announced, "Third place goes to…Lilly." Lilly graciously accepted her award.

The Mayor then announced, "Second place goes to Heather."

Heather clapped her ears and hopped up to receive her award. Evan started forward to receive the first place crown when the Mayor once more called out in his booming voice, "The new...Easter Bunny of Brookville is...Fin Bunny." Fin did a double back flip as he bounded up and accepted the crown.

Evan, stunned and embarrassed, hung his head and slunk off the stage. No bunny saw him after that. His few loyal friends looked and called for him, but they could not find him.

Now in her elder years, Ester had become quite wise. She had a feeling she might know where to find Evan.

Ester remembered how much Evan liked it when she taught him how to paint so she hopped back to the barn where her old painting place could be found.

She called out for Evan, but no answer came. Ester gently hopped into the old horse stall and softly called out once again. This time, Evan popped his head up from underneath the hay.

Ester and Evan talked for hours. Ester gave great advice and Evan saw how foolish he was for letting himself become so prideful. Ester and Evan spoke many times after that where Evan learned many valuable character lessons and finally regained his good heart. Ester encouraged Evan to compete again the next year to be the official Easter Bunny. Evan said, "NO WAY!"

Ester kept encouraging Evan, telling him it would take true humility and courage to try again. Evan finally agreed to try once more.

Evan began helping his neighbors and treating his friends with respect. He also enjoyed just having fun playing with other bunnies. Evan's actions showed that he had learned from his mistakes.

The next winter season arrived and this time Evan took the right hops. He enrolled in the Fine Bunny Academy and signed up for the Brookville Easter Bunny contest.

When the contest was held, Evan used the training and advice he received to give his best effort. A handsome and smiling Evan hopped past the judges giving a perfect bunny ear wave. His egg painting and hiding skills were the best. In fact, the results were not even close. The judges scored Evan first in every event. The finalists were selected and the moment of truth came when Evan was asked, "Why do you want to be the Easter Bunny?" Evan honestly replied, "I have been blessed with a second chance and I am humbled to be considered for the honor. If I win, I only hope to be a good representative of all the bunnies around the world."

Evan sat quietly as the Mayor stepped up to the microphone. After reading off the third and second place finishers the Mayor was ready to announce the winner. With his booming voice he shouted, "The new official Easter Bunny of Brookville is Evan…" and before he could say "Bunny", the crowd jumped up cheering loudly. The Mayor, grinning from ear to ear, placed the crown onto a very humble and honored Evan Bunny.

Pride had caused Evan to lose many friends and the first contest. After being humbled, he learned from his mistakes, regained his good heart, and showed courage to try again. In the end, Evan became a true friend and champion to all.

Way to go Evan!

Parent/Teacher Guide:

DEFINITIONS:

Pride (in this story) - Feeling superior to others. Having a higher opinion of oneself than earned. Having an, "I deserve it" attitude.

Humble – modest, respectful, courteous, without pride.

QUESTIONS TO ASK YOUR CHILD/CHILDREN OR STUDENTS:

What were the reasons Evan did not attend Easter Bunny prep school before the first contest?

Was it a wise choice by Evan to not attend Easter Bunny prep school before the first contest? Why or why not?

If you are good at something, would it help you to get more practice and training to get even better? Why?

After Evan lost the first contest, what do you think would have happened if Ester had not encouraged him to try again?

What do you think would have happened if Evan remained prideful and was not able to humble himself?

What does this statement mean: pride comes before a fall?

You may choose to have a discussion about pride, humility, failure, and success. Ask your child/children or students if they remember times when others were prideful. How did it make them feel? Ask them if they remember times when others were humble. How did it make them feel? (refer to the above definitions to help the children understand the question).

You may choose to have a conversation about failure and success. Some youth feel like they have failed or do not meet expectations. Share: even if a person does not succeed at something, they are not a failure unless they totally give up. Thomas Edison was not successful 99 times before he succeeded in inventing a light bulb that worked. What would have happened if he had never tried or had given up before his 100th attempt?

16679686R00015

Made in the USA
Charleston, SC
05 January 2013